A FOREVER HOME FOR FLUFFY

Fluffy meowed loudly and gave Mr Gregory a hard stare. Mr Gregory's lips twitched like he wanted to smile but then his eyes fell on Patch's old bowl. "No, I don't want a pet," he said, frowning. "And if I did, I'd get a proper cat, not a daft looking powder puff like this one."

HAVE YOU READ?

A FOREVER HOME FOR TILLY

A FOREVER HOME FOR PIP

A FOREVER HOME FOR LUNA

LOOK OUT FOR:

A FOREVER HOME FOR BELLA

A FOREVER HOME FOR FLUFFY

LINDA CHAPMAN

Illustrated By
Sophy Williams

nosy
crow

First published in the UK in 2020 by Nosy Crow Ltd
The Crow's Nest, 14 Baden Place
Crosby Row, London SE1 1YW

www.nosycrow.com

ISBN: 978 1 78800 797 9

A CIP catalogue record for this book will be available from the British Library.

Printed and bound in Great Britain by Clays Ltd, Elcograf S.p.A.

Papers used by Nosy Crow are made from
wood grown in sustainable forests.

MIX
Paper from
responsible sources
FSC® C018072

1 3 5 7 9 10 8 6 4 2

To Angel.
A real angel pony.
Ears pricked, eyes sparkling,
you're galloping with
the unicorns now.

CHAPTER 1

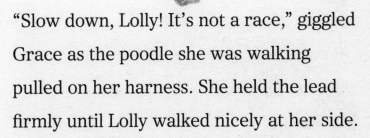

"Slow down, Lolly! It's not a race," giggled
Grace as the poodle she was walking
pulled on her harness. She held the lead
firmly until Lolly walked nicely at her side.

"Coco can't wait to get to the park
either," said Jack, who was walking a

    1

brown-and-white spaniel. "Look at her ears. She's going so fast it's making them flap."

Grace grinned. "They look like wings. Are you trying to fly, Coco?"

It was the first day of the May half-term and nine-year-old twins Grace and Jack Taylor were helping out at Top Dog, their mother's doggy day care and boarding business.

"Lucky for me that you're not busy today," said Mum, who was walking four other dogs. "This is the busiest week I've had in ages. I think the whole town has gone on holiday together."

"Not old Mr Grumpy Pants," said Grace, nodding at an elderly gentleman standing in the large garden of a bungalow a few doors down from the Taylors. The garden wrapped all the way around the front and sides of the building. There was a shed on the left-hand side of it and a path on the right which led to the front door. The flower beds were full of colourful roses and the lawn was mown in neat stripes. The man was inspecting it. "Look at the way he's scowling at the grass," Grace went on. "I bet he's telling it off for not

   3

growing in a straight line!"

"I like Mr Gregory's garden," said Jack as Coco and Lolly pulled them towards the hedge. "It's really tidy and the stripy grass is fun. And look at the bird table over there. It's full of tasty bird snacks. See the robin? It's loving those seeds!" He pushed his dark hair out of his eyes.

The robin flew up from the bird table. Mr Gregory spun round and spotted the twins. "Keep those dogs away from my garden!" he ordered crossly. "They're scaring the birds."

"His grumpy face is scaring the birds, more like," Grace whispered to Jack. "The dogs are miles away from his stupid bird table."

"Shh, Grace! That's rude," said Jack, glancing at Mr Gregory, worried that he might have heard.

"So? I don't like people who don't like dogs," muttered Grace.

Their mum joined them at the hedge. "Good morning, Mr Gregory. What a lovely sunny day!"

"Hello, Mrs Taylor," Mr Gregory said gruffly. "Yes, it is a beautiful morning. I hope you enjoy your walk."

"See? He's not so bad, Grace," Jack said as they carried on along the road. "And he does like dogs really. Don't you remember

Patch, his old Jack Russell? When Patch got ill last summer, Mr Gregory put an umbrella up in the garden so that Patch could sit outside in the shade."

"I'd forgotten that," Mum said, nodding. "Mr Gregory was always talking to that dog or grooming him. He must really miss Patch. Perhaps he'd be able give a small dog a forever home, the next time you get one in."

Grace and Jack had their own pet rehoming service called Forever Homes. They took in unwanted cats and dogs and cared for them until a home could be found with a perfect new owner.

"No way!" Grace vowed. Mr Gregory was far too grumpy to make a perfect owner for a Forever Homes dog!

Lolly wagged her tail excitedly as they entered the park. A woman came hurrying towards them, chasing after four young children on trikes and scooters.

"Everyone, STOP!" cried the lady, catching sight of the Taylors. "Just for a minute. I want to ask that lady with all the dogs a question."

One of the younger children ran over. "Can I stroke the doggies, please?" she asked.

"Yes, you can, thank you for asking," said Mrs Taylor, making the dogs sit. "That's lovely stroking – and well done the rest of you, too." she added as the other children crowded around, gently stroking the dogs and giggling as the dogs licked their hands.

"Hi there," said the lady. "My name's Helen – Helen Nixon. I hope you don't mind me stopping you, but you look like you know all about dogs and I need some

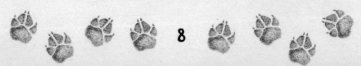

8

advice. I'm thinking of getting a dog. We bought a kitten a couple of months ago but it's not working out. Don't get me wrong, Fluffy is gorgeous. She's five months old and very cute, but . . ." Mrs Nixon lowered her voice. "She also likes hunting. She keeps bringing mice in from the garden and sometimes they're still alive." She pulled a face. "It's a bit horrible and the kids are getting upset. I think a dog might suit us better."

Grace immediately pricked up her ears. If Mrs Nixon wasn't getting on with her cat then maybe Forever Homes could help her. She widened her eyes at Jack and he nodded. Grace grinned. She loved the fact that she and Jack often had exactly the same thought. It was one of the best things

about being twins!

Mum smiled sympathetically. "It does sound like a cat might not be the right pet for your family, but are you sure you could cope with a dog?"

"We all love walking, we've got a big garden and I'm home all day. My great-aunt can't manage her Labrador any more. He's good with kids and well trained. I wondered about taking him in for her and finding a new home for Fluffy."

"That sounds like a very good plan," Mum said.

Mrs Nixon looked relieved. "That's what I thought too."

"What will you do with Fluffy?" Grace burst out. "If you want a new home for her, my brother and I could help."

   11

"Yes," Jack added. "Grace and I run a pet rehoming service called Forever Homes."

"We find unwanted pets their perfect forever homes," Grace said.

Mrs Nixon gave their mum a questioning look.

"It's true," said Mum. "The twins have rehomed quite a few dogs and cats."

"Last month, we rehomed a cockapoo puppy called Tilly," said Jack. "But right now we haven't got any animals to look after."

"Really?" said Mrs Nixon. "Well, if you would help with Fluffy, I'd be very grateful. I do want her to go to a good home where she'll be loved."

"Absolutely." Mum smiled back at her.

"If you're happy for Grace and Jack to rehome her then perhaps you'd like to bring her round. We can have a chat about dogs at the same time and I can give you some advice on settling a new dog in."

"That would be brilliant," said Mrs Nixon. "How soon can I come over?"

"We're free this afternoon," said Jack. "I think I've got a card somewhere with our details on." He rummaged in his pocket, pulling out a marble, an old sweet, a football card and finally a Forever Homes business card. "Here you are. We can see you any time after two o'clock."

"Wonderful. I'll bring Fluffy then," said Mrs Nixon, beaming. "Oh, this has all worked out perfectly! I'm so glad I stopped you."

"We'll see you later," said Mum as she and the twins set off with the dogs again.

"A new pet to rehome!" said Jack happily.

"A kitten!" said Grace. Excitement fizzed through her. "I really can't wait until this afternoon!"

CHAPTER 2

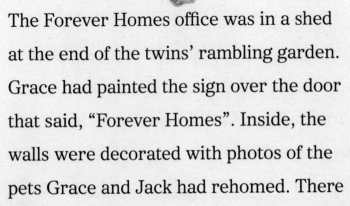

The Forever Homes office was in a shed
at the end of the twins' rambling garden.
Grace had painted the sign over the door
that said, "Forever Homes". Inside, the
walls were decorated with photos of the
pets Grace and Jack had rehomed. There

   15

was a desk, a water bowl and a crate of dog and cat toys. A little after two o'clock, Grace and Jack were tidying up when there was a knock.

Grace opened the door to her mother and Mrs Nixon, who was carrying a plastic pet carrier. "Is that Fluffy?" said Grace eagerly, peering in at the little white kitten. "She's just a huge white ball!"

The fluff ball moved and two bright green eyes stared back at Grace.

"She's adorable," breathed Grace. Fluffy had the pinkest nose and long white whiskers that twitched delicately. Grace longed to take her out of the pet carrier and give her a cuddle. She waited impatiently as Jack checked the little cat in, writing her details in the big blue Forever Homes notebook and getting Mrs Nixon to sign a piece of paper officially giving Fluffy to them. When he'd finished, Mum took Mrs Nixon away to talk to her about settling her new dog into the family.

"At last!" said Grace. "Shut the door, Jack. I'm letting Fluffy out."

Jack closed the shed door firmly and

checked the windows were shut too.

"We're going to have to be very careful. If Fluffy gets into the garden she could easily jump over the fence and get lost. It takes a while before cats recognise new houses as their homes."

Grace undid the pet carrier and stayed quite still as Fluffy stretched forward to sniff at Grace's fingers.

"See? I'm very friendly." Grace encouraged the kitten by wiggling her fingers.

Fluffy meowed and stalked confidently out of the carrier. She rubbed her face against Grace's hand. "Oooh!" Grace murmured. "You're so cute. Everyone's going to want to give you a new forever home!"

"Let's do the personality test," said Jack.
All animals who came to Forever Homes
took a personality test. It helped the twins
match the animal to a suitable new owner.
Jack took a ball out of the crate of toys and
rolled it across the floor. The bell inside
tinkled as it rolled. Fluffy watched it with
a bored expression
then rubbed her
head against
Grace's leg.

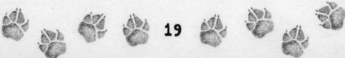

"She's not very playful," said Jack, making a note on the test sheet.

"Let's do the cuddle test next," said Grace.

"Not yet, Grace!" said Jack. "Let's try her with another toy first." He set a plastic fish in front of Fluffy and wiggled it from side to side. Fluffy watched it, her tail twitching. Then she pounced, snatching the fish from Jack with her claws.

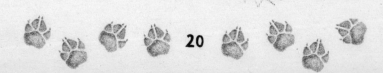

"She's got very fast reactions," said Jack, writing it down. "OK, now let's see if she likes cuddles."

It was the moment Grace had been waiting for. She scooped Fluffy up. The kitten snuggled into her chest, rubbing against Grace's chin. Grace kissed the top of her head. "She definitely likes being cuddled! Here, you try, Jack."

He took her and Fluffy snuggled into his arms. Jack smiled. "She's so soft. Let's try grooming her. Can you pass the special brush for long-haired cats? It should be in the cupboard."

Grace found the brush. It had a mixture of long and short wire teeth and was great for brushing out tangles. While Jack held Fluffy, Grace ran the brush through the kitten's long coat, brushing a small section of fur at a time. "Her coat is really lovely. It feels like silk. Mrs Nixon must have groomed her every day to keep it this nice."

"Fluffy seems to like being groomed," said Jack.

"She does! Can you hear her purring? She sounds just like a car engine. She's going to need a family who doesn't mind cat hair though," Grace added, realising her jeans were covered in long white fur. She took Fluffy from her brother so he could write some more notes on the test sheet.

"So, she needs to be with an owner who is prepared to spend time grooming her, who doesn't mind cat hair and who

   22

doesn't mind when she brings mice inside, so probably a home without young children," said Jack, reading his notes back. "She's not very playful but she's friendly and loves a cuddle. Last thing, we need to find out is how she is with dogs. You stay here. I'll go and fetch Tiny."

Tiny was the family's enormous German Shepherd cross. He was a gentle giant and he loved cats. Jack led him into the shed, stopping a short distance away from Fluffy who was dozing, all snuggled up on Grace's lap.

Tiny's nose twitched with interest as he caught Fluffy's scent. Spotting her in Grace's lap, he lay down. Fluffy's green eyes opened wide and with a hiss of warning she fixed Tiny with an unblinking look. Tiny made himself flatter by pressing further into the floor, resting his nose on his paws to show Fluffy that he meant her no harm.

Fluffy stalked towards Tiny as if he was a giant mouse. When the animals were almost nose to nose, Fluffy raised a paw and swiped the air just above Tiny's nose. Tiny grunted in surprise. Fluffy jumped

   24

back. Tiny stayed very still, his face resting on his paws. Fluffy walked all around him and then climbed on his back. Tiny didn't move as Fluffy confidently settled on his head and meowed.

"Aw, that's so sweet!" said Grace.

"You're such a good boy, Tiny."

He wagged his tail but stayed very still.

   25

"I think we can definitely say Fluffy likes dogs," Grace went on.

"And is happy to boss them around," added Jack. "So, do we know anyone who wants a cat like Fluffy?"

Grace shook her head. "Not that I can think of, but I'm sure we'll find someone." She stroked the little kitten. "The perfect owner is out there waiting for you, Fluffy."

Jack grinned at her. "And we're going to find them!"

CHAPTER 3

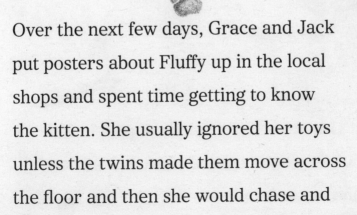

Over the next few days, Grace and Jack
put posters about Fluffy up in the local
shops and spent time getting to know
the kitten. She usually ignored her toys
unless the twins made them move across
the floor and then she would chase and

pounce. Most of the time she spent
either demanding cuddles or sleeping.
Her favourite spots were in the kitchen,
stretched out on the window seat snoozing
in the sunlight, or snuggled up to Tiny.

The twins had a couple of people call,
but they both wanted short-haired cats
and weren't interested when they heard

   28

how much grooming Fluffy needed.

A week after Fluffy had arrived, the twins came in from their karate lesson starving and ready for tea. Amelia, their thirteen-year-old sister, was in the kitchen, listening to music on her phone with Fluffy curled on her lap, while Dad was putting the plates out on the side as he got ready to dish up dinner.

"Where's Ollie?" asked Mum, dropping her car key in the dresser drawer.

"I'm here," said Ollie, the twins' seventeen-year-old brother. He pushed open the door and came inside. "I've just got back from the funfair."

"Boring," said Amelia. "My friends and I went but the rides were totally lame. The ghost train broke down and we had to get out and walk through giant fake spiders' webs hanging from the ceiling. They weren't even a tiny bit scary."

"Oooh, you're so brave, Amelia," Ollie teased. "Doesn't anything scare you?"

"Only your face," Amelia retorted.

"Amelia," warned Mum. "That's not very nice."

Ollie winked at Grace. She watched him take something from his pocket and set it on the floor. "Watch out, Amelia. A rat!" he shouted.

"What? Where?" Amelia twisted round so fast she tipped Fluffy from her lap. "Aaaaah!" she squealed as something brown and furry shot across the kitchen towards her. Fluffy sprang lightning fast, pouncing on the rat and snatching it up in

her mouth.

"Fluffy!" cried Jack as she shook it hard and then pinned it to the ground.

Grace could hardly bear to look. She knew it was natural for cats to kill rats and mice but she didn't want to have to watch. She peeked between her fingers as the rat started to make a weird buzzing sound.

It's not real! Grace realised with a rush of relief. *It's just a wind-up toy.*

Fluffy carried the toy rat proudly over to Amelia and dumped it in her lap.

"Gross!" Amelia shrieked, jumping up.

"Don't you like Mr Ratty?" said Ollie. He wiggled the toy under Amelia's nose, making her shriek even louder and climb up on her chair.

"Amelia, stop it," Mum said, her

shoulders heaving with laughter.

Dad was chuckling too. "It's only a toy, Amelia. It's not a real rat."

"It's clockwork! I won it at the fair." Ollie could hardly get his words out for laughing. "Isn't it brilliant? It's so lifelike."

"I hate you!" Amelia told him, climbing off the chair crossly.

"Mrs Nixon's right, Fluffy is an excellent mouser," Jack said to Grace. "And she's not afraid to tackle rats either!" Fluffy stalked around looking very proud of herself.

"Did you see how much she loved catching it?" said Grace. "We need to find her a home where her mousing skills can come in useful."

"Maybe a farm?" Jack suggested.

Mum raised her eyebrows. "With all that hair?"

"I guess not," admitted Jack.

Fluffy jumped up beside the sink and stood by the cold water tap. She meowed. "What does she want?" said Mum.

"That's her way of saying she wants a drink," said Grace, getting up and turning the tap on. Fluffy lapped the water from the tap as it poured into the sink. "She's decided she doesn't like drinking from her water bowl. She likes people to turn the tap on for her," Grace explained.

"You're a real princess, aren't you, Fluffy?" Mum teased, stroking the kitten behind her ears. "You're going to need an owner who's happy to be bossed around."

Jack frowned. "I don't think it's going to be as easy to find a home for her as we thought. She needs someone who will give her lots of attention, who doesn't mind when she catches mice, who's happy to groom her—"

"And cuddle her," said Grace, scooping the kitten up. "We'll find you the perfect home, don't worry, Fluffy," she promised.

The next day, the twins got a phone call from a young woman called Tina Samson who sounded like she might be ideal. She worked from home and loved animals.

She hadn't had a cat before but had owned
long-haired guinea pigs and was used to
grooming them. After chatting to her on
the phone, the twins agreed to take Fluffy
round to meet her and to see if her house
was suitable. Their mum was busy so Ollie
took them – he'd passed his driving test six
months ago.

Tina was slim with short, dark hair and
a wide smile. "Oh, what a sweet kitty!" she
exclaimed, peering through the bars of the
carrier. "I love kittens. I've always wanted
one. I just love animals so much!"

Jack and Grace exchanged hopeful looks.
Ollie came in with them and they checked
the house. It seemed fine for a cat. The
terraced house was on a very quiet street
and there was a garden at the back.

"Can we get her out?" Tina asked the twins.

"Sure," said Jack. He opened the carrier door and Fluffy stalked out.

"She's adorable," said Tina. She picked Fluffy up and the kitten purred.

Grace crossed her fingers. Everything was going so well! Just then, her eye was caught by something moving on the far side of the room. A large spider came scuttling out from behind the sofa. "Jack!" she said warningly as she saw Fluffy stiffen all over.

Tina smiled, misunderstanding Grace's alarm. "Are you scared of spiders, Grace? Don't worry, I'll catch it and put it outside. I never kill spiders – I never kill anything. Not beetles or wasps or – *Argh*!" She broke

36

off with a scream as Fluffy leapt from her arms.

In the blink of an eye, Fluffy had pounced on the spider, tossing it up in the air and back to the floor. She patted it with her front paws but it didn't move. With a happy meow, Fluffy picked it up and carried it across the room and dropped it proudly on Tina's foot.

 37

Tina screamed even more loudly than Amelia had with the toy rat. "She's a killer!" she gasped, backing away and pointing at Fluffy. "That kitten's a vicious killer!"

Grace, Jack and Ollie made a hasty exit.

"Definitely not the right home," Jack said as they got into the car with Fluffy.

"Definitely not," Grace agreed with a sigh.

CHAPTER 4

When they got home, Dad asked them
to walk to the shop and buy some milk.
Leaving Fluffy snoozing on the window
seat, they headed out. They took a tennis
ball and threw it between them as they
walked down the street.

   39

"Maybe someone else will ring up soon," said Jack.

Grace giggled. "Tina really wasn't right for Fluffy, was she? *That kitten's a vicious killer!*" she mimicked as she threw the ball to Jack.

Jack was so busy laughing that he missed the ball. It flew over Mr Gregory's hedge, bounced on the grass and hit the bottom of the shed door with a bang.

"Oi, you young hooligans!" Mr Gregory appeared from the side of the shed. "You can stop that right now or I'll be talking to your parents!"

"Sorry, Mr Gregory," Jack apologised in alarm. "It was just an accident."

"We didn't mean to hit your shed," said Grace. Under her breath, she added,

40

"Mr Grumpy Pants."

Mr Gregory examined his shed door, his face reddening. "There's a hole! You've made a hole in my shed!"

Grace went hot with indignation. How could such a small ball make a hole like that? It hadn't even hit the shed that hard. "We didn't. . ." she started, then something small and furry scampered through the hole and dived into Mr Gregory's roses.

"A mouse!" exclaimed Jack. "Did you see it? I bet that mouse made the hole, not our ball."

Mr Gregory stared at the rose bushes in astonishment. "I've got mice! Mice!" He shook his head. "Well, that's all I need, mice in my shed, eating my plant seeds and whatnot." He harrumphed angrily. "I'll have to do something about that."

"What about Fluffy?" Jack whispered to Grace. "Could Mr Gregory—"

"No!" she hissed. She knew exactly what Jack was about to say and there was no way a grumpy old man like Mr Gregory would be the right owner for a cute kitten like Fluffy.

Mr Gregory glanced at them, the anger fading from his expression. "All right,

maybe it wasn't your ball that made the hole. You can come and fetch it."

Jack and Grace went in through the gate and retrieved the ball as Mr Gregory slowly bent to inspect the hole in the door.

"Look, an old dog bowl!" Jack hissed, nudging Grace. "Remember what Mum said? Mr Gregory might not be right for Fluffy but he might want to rehome a dog the next time we get a small one in. Let's ask him while we're here."

"Jack, no!" Grace said, horrified, but it was too late to stop him. He had picked up the bowl and was already approaching the old man.

"Excuse me, Mr Gregory, but my sister Grace and I take in unwanted dogs and cats for rehoming. You used to have a

    43

Jack Russell, didn't you? Would you be interested in giving a new dog a forever home, if we take one in?"

Grace saw Mr Gregory straighten up. He gave Jack a gruff smile.

"No, lad, I wouldn't be able to rehome a dog. It's my arthritis, see. I can't walk too far these days. It wouldn't be fair to take a dog on now. I couldn't exercise one." Mr Gregory took Patch's old bowl from Jack, holding it carefully in his hands. His eyes looked sad. "Animals!" he said, shaking his head and talking almost to himself. "They're expensive. They make a mess. They're a huge responsibility and then they leave you too soon and break your heart." He looked up and saw the twins and his smile vanished. "You're still

here! You've got your ball so off you go now. Shoo!" Mr Gregory waved Grace and Jack away with his hands.

"We're going," said Grace, dragging Jack out of the garden.

As they went out on to the road, she shook her head at him. "Honestly, Jack! Mr Gregory's so bad-tempered. There's no way he'd be a good owner for one of our animals."

"But, Grace, he seems sad," Jack argued as they carried on walking to the shops. "He obviously loved his old dog. You know, I think Mr Gregory might be a bit like Fluffy."

Grace stared. Was her brother nuts?

"They're both not what they seem. She looks sweet and cuddly, but she's also a

    45

fierce hunting cat," Jack explained.
"Mr Gregory's the opposite. He's grumpy
on the outside, but I bet he's a big softie
really."

Grace snorted with laughter. "You're
wrong and you're never going to make me
like him and we're never – ever – going to
rehome an animal to him!"

When Grace and Jack returned with
the milk, Mum was having a tea break
with Dad. Grace made them laugh by
recounting how Jack had lost his ball and
doing an impression of Mr Gregory and
the mouse.

"Honestly, Grace, are you sure you're
not exaggerating a teensy bit?" Mum said
with a smile. "Jack's right, Mr Gregory is

actually kind under his gruff exterior. He's always feeding the birds and he absolutely adored that Jack Russell of his. Nothing was too much trouble for him when it came to Patch, in fact—"

There was a knock on the door. Mum broke off to answer it. An older lady with curly hair was on the doorstep. "Hello, my name's Pam," she said. "I was in the newsagent's and I saw your poster that said you have a kitten that needs a home."

"We do," Mum said. "It's my children you need to talk to, though. They're in charge of finding the right home for her. Come in."

Pam stepped inside. Tiny got up and Pam gave him some fuss then greeted Grace and Jack with a smile. "Is that the kitten? She's beautiful!" she said, spotting Fluffy on the window seat.

"Would you mind if we ask you some questions?" said Jack.

"That's absolutely fine," said Pam.

Mum left them to it and Pam told them she lived on her own and wanted a friendly cat who liked cuddles. "My grandchildren sleep over quite often. The youngest is just nine months, the middle one is three and the eldest is six."

Grace and Jack looked at each other.

"I'm really sorry, I don't think you're going to be suitable," said Jack politely. "You'd be a lovely owner for a different cat, but Fluffy is a brilliant mouser and she likes to bring her prey indoors. It might upset your grandchildren."

   48

Pam stared at Fluffy in surprise. "She looks so cute and cuddly! I'd never have guessed! Oh dear. She's definitely not the cat for me, in that case. I'm sorry to have wasted your time."

"Don't worry at all. Thank you for calling in," said Grace.

Grace moved to let Pam out but as she did so, she accidentally trod on Tiny's tail. Tiny jumped to his feet with a surprised yelp. "Oh, Tiny, I'm sorry!" said Grace, throwing her arms around his neck.

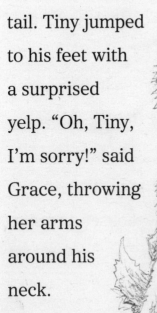

"I'll see myself out," called Pam as Jack
went over to stroke Tiny too. Tiny wagged
his tail, enjoying the sudden fuss.

"Here, I'll get you a treat to say sorry,
Tiny," said Grace, getting a bone-shaped
dog biscuit from
a tin on the side.

"It's such a shame Pam wasn't right for Fluffy," sighed Jack as Tiny happily crunched on the biscuit.

Grace nodded. "If only we could train Fluffy not to hunt, it would make her much easier to rehome." She looked around. "Where is Fluffy?"

"Oh no!" Jack gasped. "Look! The door's ajar! Pam can't have shut it properly."

Grace ran to the door. But there was no sign of Fluffy in the courtyard. Grace's heart began to hammer against her chest. "She's not here, Jack! She's gone!"

CHAPTER 5

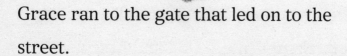

Grace ran to the gate that led on to the street.

"Grace, where are you going?" shouted Jack. "We can't go out without telling Mum or Dad!"

Just then Ollie came into the kitchen

with his toy rat. He held it up to Jack and said in a squeaky voice, "Help, I'm Hatty the Ratty. Hide me from the nasty catty."

"Stop it, Ollie!" Jack growled. "Fluffy's gone. She got out a few minutes ago!"

"Really?" Ollie was suddenly serious. He put the rat down. "You're sure she's not in the courtyard?"

"Yes," said Jack, running out.

Ollie followed him. "She can't have gone far. I'll help you check the street, but first I'll let Mum know we're going out."

The twins hurried outside. Ollie quickly joined them. "Mum, Dad and Amelia are coming to help. I told them we'd go this way and they're going to look in the other direction," said Ollie, setting off along the street with Grace and Jack. "We'll find her," he reassured them.

But although they looked and looked, they didn't find any sign of Fluffy. In the end they had to go home.

"Don't worry," said Ollie. "She'll come back when she's hungry."

"Not if she's lost," Grace said anxiously.

"Cats have got a really good sense of direction," Jack said, though he didn't sound convinced.

Fluffy still hadn't returned by dinner time. Dad had cooked his special homemade pizza, but Grace could barely eat. What if Fluffy was hurt or stuck somewhere? She hated to think of the little kitten lost, scared and alone.

"Can Jack and I go and have one last look before we go to bed?" she begged.

"All right," said Mum. "But no further than the top of the street."

The twins hurried out. They peered under hedges and looked over fences.

"There's Mr Gregory. I wonder if he's seen Fluffy. Let's go and ask him," said Jack.

"Jack, no!" said Grace. "He'll only yell at us."

But Jack was already walking towards the elderly man's gate. Grace ran after him. Mr Gregory was by his shed.

As they went through the gate, Grace saw a furry white ball of fluff beside Mr Gregory. It was Fluffy! Purring ecstatically, she was rubbing her head against Mr Gregory's legs as he tickled her behind her ears.

Noticing the twins, Mr Gregory straightened up. "You two again. What do you want now?"

"You've got Fluffy!" Jack exclaimed, hurrying across the lawn. "We thought she was lost."

"This cat?" said Mr Gregory.

Grace nodded. "We're looking after her and trying to find her a new home."

"She was in my shed," said Mr Gregory. "She must have squeezed in through that hole the mice made. I'll board it up tomorrow."

Grace hesitated. There was no denying how gentle the old man had been when he was fussing the kitten. Maybe Jack was right and he would be a good owner after all. She glanced at her twin. Jack grinned

and nodded and she knew they were thinking the same thing.

"Mr Gregory, would you like a cat?" Grace said impulsively.

"She's a great mouser," Jack added.

"And you wouldn't have to walk her," said Grace. "She's less work than a dog, but just as friendly."

As if she knew she was being talked about, Fluffy meowed loudly and gave Mr Gregory a hard stare. Mr Gregory's lips twitched like he wanted to smile. He reached down his hand but then his eyes fell on Patch's old bowl and he seemed to stop himself. "No, I don't want a pet," he said, frowning. "And if I did, I'd get a proper cat, not a daft-looking powder puff like this one. Now hurry up and get out of

 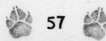

here. I'm busy."

Grace ran over and lifted Fluffy into
her arms. The little cat purred loudly, her
silky body throbbing. Grace scowled at
Mr Gregory. "Fluffy
is a proper cat!"
she said hotly.

"Fluffy!" Mr Gregory snorted. "What sort of name's that?"

"We're going now," said Jack hastily, grabbing Grace's arm. "Thanks for finding her, Mr Gregory. If you do decide you'd like to offer Fluffy a home, then come and see us."

"I won't," Mr Gregory grunted. "Now go!"

Grace stomped out of the garden with Jack hurrying behind her. "I really don't like that man!" she declared. "You *are* a proper cat, Fluffy, and Fluffy is a lovely name. Don't you take any notice of him."

Jack took one last look at Mr Gregory, who was watching them. Then he hurried after Grace.

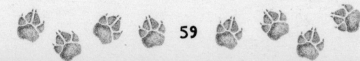

CHAPTER 6

Mum, Dad, Ollie and Amelia were all in the kitchen when the twins got home. "You found her!" Mum jumped up, taking Fluffy from Grace. Dad fetched the cat bowl and filled it with food while Ollie and Amelia crowded round, stroking Fluffy. The kitten

purred, loving all the attention. Jack recounted how they'd found her.

"You know," he finished thoughtfully, "Fluffy really would be the perfect pet for Mr Gregory, if only he'd give her a chance."

"He wouldn't be perfect at all. He said she wasn't a proper cat!" Grace exploded.

"I don't think he meant it," said Jack. "You were too busy talking to Fluffy when we left to notice, but I saw his face. He looked sad. I think he'd love a cat really, and he needs a good mouser."

"I suppose Fluffy isn't the sort of cat a man like Mr Gregory might naturally choose," said Mum. "But maybe you can persuade him to change his mind and look beneath the surface."

   61

"If anyone can, you two can," said Dad, putting the food down for Fluffy. She wriggled out of Mum's arms and started to eat hungrily.

"Grace?" Jack said, looking at her. "I really think we should try."

Grace considered it. She couldn't deny that Mr Gregory had looked very happy when he'd been stroking Fluffy and he'd been very gentle with the kitten. He had clearly loved Patch a lot and been a very good owner. Maybe he would be right for Fluffy after all. "OK," she said, giving in. "I don't know

how we'll make him want her though. He
didn't seem too keen."

They all looked at Fluffy. She had
finished her food and was looking round
for something to do. She spotted Tiny's tail
waving on the floor and pounced on it.

"No, don't do that!" said Jack quickly.
"Poor Tiny."

"Here, have this instead," said Grace,
spotting the rat. She wound it up and put it
on the floor.

"Seriously? Do you have to?" said
Amelia with a shudder.

"Fluffy likes it," protested Grace. "Go
and get it, Fluffy!"

Fluffy darted after the clockwork rat, pouncing on it, then holding it down.

"If Mr Gregory saw you do that he wouldn't say you were just a silly fluff ball," Grace said. Her eyes widened suddenly. "Oh, wow! I think I've just had the perfect idea!"

The next morning, after breakfast, Grace and Jack hurried round to Mr Gregory's. Jack had the clockwork rat in his pocket and Grace was carrying Fluffy. Mr Gregory was in his garden, beside a wheelbarrow. While Grace kept Fluffy distracted, Jack wound the rat up and, quietly opening Mr Gregory's gate, he set it on the ground. The rat scuttled off down the path. Mr Gregory looked

up to see where the rattling noise was coming from. "What on earth –? A rat!" he exclaimed.

Grace put Fluffy down. Like a flash, Fluffy raced after the rat. She pounced, bringing it down and holding it tight. The clockwork rat spluttered and stopped. Fluffy picked it up in her mouth, proudly stalked over to Mr Gregory and dropped it at his feet.

Mr Gregory stared at the toy, his brow furrowed. He picked it up. "What the—"

"It's just a pretend rat, Mr Gregory," said Grace, hurrying into the garden. "We brought it to show you how good at catching rats and mice Fluffy is."

"*Meow!*" agreed Fluffy, weaving around Mr Gregory's legs.

"Well, she's certainly fast, I'll give her that," he admitted with a frown.

"She's a brilliant mouser," said Jack. "She's really fierce."

"And that's why lots of people don't want her," said Grace. "They don't want a cat who catches so many mice. They don't like it."

Mr Gregory looked down at Fluffy thoughtfully. "So, no one wants her."

"No," said Grace.

"I'd be doing you a favour by taking her in?" Mr Gregory said.

"Yes!" the twins said together.

Mr Gregory picked Fluffy up. "Hmmm. Well, I can see you're an excellent mouser. It seems you're not as precious as you look. What would you say to coming to live

   66

with me? Eh?"

"Yes!" squealed Grace.

Jack nudged her and gave her a warning look. "It would be great if you would give her a home, Mr Gregory. We'd just need to ask you a few questions first to check you're completely suitable."

"It's how Forever Homes works," Grace put in. "We have to be absolutely sure that our animals are going to be living in a home that's safe and right for them."

Mr Gregory's bushy eyebrows met in a scowl. "What if I don't want to answer a bunch of nosy questions?"

Jack hesitated. "Then I'm afraid we can't let you have Fluffy."

Mr Gregory shook his head. "The cheek of it! I've had dogs for fifty years. I think

I know how to look after a cat!"

"I'm sure you do, Mr Gregory, but we do need to check," said Jack.

"No!" declared Mr Gregory. "I'm not standing for it. I don't want to answer questions. You can find another home for your cat." And muttering angrily, he stomped back to his roses.

CHAPTER 7

Grace and Jack exchanged dismayed
looks. Grace felt like crying. This wasn't
how her plan was supposed to work out.

"*Meow!*" Fluffy walked after Mr Gregory
but stopped when he didn't turn back.
An indignant look crossed her face and

her whiskers quivered. "*Meow!*" she said bossily.

Mr Gregory still didn't glance back.

Fluffy trotted over and jumped into the empty wheelbarrow beside him. She fixed

him with a look and meowed very loudly again.

"Go on! Away with you!" he said, waving a hand at her but his voice, though stern, wasn't harsh. "Go on, cat! Go away!"

Fluffy jumped down and pressed against his legs. "*Meow! Meow!*" she insisted, looking up at him with her big green eyes.

Grace saw Mr Gregory's expression start to soften. "What do you think you're doing, you daft thing? I just told you to go."

"Fluffy tends to do what she wants," Grace put in. "She's a bit of a princess and she can be very bossy."

To her surprise, Mr Gregory chuckled. "Patch was just the same. He always let me know when he thought it was walk and

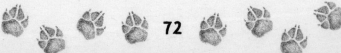

dinner time. Maybe we are suited after all." He picked Fluffy up and she cuddled into his arms. He cleared his throat. "You know, I might have been a bit hasty," he said to the twins. "It was all this talk about questions. I'm a private person, see. I'm not one for talking about myself but I can see how you need to make sure that the cat's going to a good home. It's reasonable enough. What do you want to know?"

Grace and Jack beamed at each other. "Not that much," said Jack. "You've had pets before so you know they need to see the vet regularly for check-ups and have their vaccinations."

Mr Gregory nodded.

"And you'll be happy to groom Fluffy?" said Grace.

"Aye, that's fine. And I don't mind a bit of hair about the house. I'm in most of the time so she'll have company and there's a sunny window ledge that Patch used to like to sit on. I'm sure she'll make herself at home there," said Mr Gregory.

"Perfect!" said Grace.

"The street outside is quiet without much traffic, which is great, and your garden looks suitable," said Jack, glancing around. His eyes fell on the bird table, laden with fat balls and nutty snacks. His face fell. "Apart from the bird table. Fluffy's a brilliant climber. She'll be able to get up there and she'll scare the birds away. Is that going to be a problem?"

Mr Gregory sucked in a breath.

Grace bit her lip. She knew Mr Gregory

 74

loved the birds visiting his garden. Would he give them up for a cat?

She saw him hesitate before a smile crossed his face.

"I've got it!" he burst out, making Fluffy jump. "I'll get a plastic tube to cover the bird table's pole. She won't be able to dig her claws into that," he added, his face breaking into a grin. "It'll be too slippery for you, won't it?" he said to the cat. "Besides," he continued, talking to Fluffy as if she had answered him, "you're going to be so busy chasing the mice out of my shed that you won't have time to scare my birds."

"That's a brilliant idea," said Jack.

"We can help you fix up the tube, if you like," Grace offered.

Mr Gregory stared at her in surprise. "Well, that would be lovely. Thank you. And as for you. . ." his eyes were soft as he smiled down at Fluffy. "I'll go into town this afternoon to get the things you need, like a comfy cat bed, a litter tray and bowls. I'd better get some food too. Now, what do you like to eat? Fresh chicken, I bet! None of that boring old tinned food for a cat like you."

Fluffy's ears pricked up as if she understood. "*Meeeeeow!*" she agreed.

"She says that's perfect," Grace chuckled.

On a sunny day, a week later, Grace and Jack called in on Mr Gregory with some cookies baked by their dad and a bag of

fishy treats for Fluffy. As they walked up the path to the door, Jack nudged Grace's arm. "I bet you never thought Fluffy would end up with Mr Gregory. It just goes to show, you should never judge someone only by their looks."

"I know," said Grace, blushing slightly. "Mr Gregory seemed so grumpy, but he's not. He's actually really kind."

"Exactly." Jack pointed at the kitchen window where a white kitten was stretched out on the window ledge, eyes half-closed, soaking up the sunlight. "And look at Fluffy now. She doesn't look like a fierce mouse hunter."

"She looks very happy." Grace couldn't stop grinning. "We really did it, Jack. We found Fluffy her *puuurrfect* forever home."

Jack nodded as they high-fived. "We did, and now I can't wait to find another pet who needs our help."

"Me too!" Grace nodded. "I hope it's very, very soon!"

Are you the **CAT'S** whiskers with your kitten know-how?

Answer these questions to find out!

1   YOU HAVE JUST GOT A NEW KITTEN.
     WHAT SHOULD YOU DO WHEN YOU FIRST
     GET IT HOME?

     a) Keep the kitten indoors while
     it gets used to its new home

     b) Leave the kitten out in the
     garden so it can explore

     c) Take the kitten out to visit all
     your friends

2   HOW SHOULD YOU PICK UP A KITTEN?

a) With one hand only. Kittens don't like to be touched

b) With two hands, one under its chest and the other under its back legs

c) Tempt your kitten into a carrier before you lift it

3   WHAT SHOULD YOU FEED YOUR KITTEN?

a) Apples

b) Tinned, dried or fresh cat food

c) Spaghetti

4   HOW OFTEN SHOULD YOU GIVE YOUR KITTEN WATER TO DRINK?

a) Once a day

b) Twice a day

c) Leave fresh water out at all times

5　WHERE SHOULD YOUR KITTEN SLEEP?

a) In its own cat bed in a special place that's out of the way in the house

b) On your bed

c) Under a table

6　HOW OFTEN SHOULD YOU BRUSH YOUR KITTEN'S FUR?

a) Never

b) Occasionally if it has short hair. Every day if it has long hair.

c) Once a year

ANSWERS ON PAGE 89

JACK'S FACT FILE

NAME: Jack Samuel Taylor

AGE: nine

LIKES: ANIMALS! Making lists, notebooks, karate, cross-country running

DISLIKES: untidy places and bullies

FAVOURITE COLOUR: red

FAVOURITE SCHOOL SUBJECT: science and PE

FAVOURITE FOODS: burgers, Dad's chocolate-dipped flapjacks

FAVOURITE ANIMAL: cats and dogs

FAVOURITE JOKE:

Q: Why should you be careful when it's raining cats and dogs?

A: Because you might step in a poodle!

DREAM JOB: wild-animal vet or a zookeeper

WHAT CAT WOULD YOU BE: A Scottish wildcat because they're smart, agile and very independent. I'm good at running, climbing and organising things. I love camping and it would be great fun to live in a forest.

COOL
CAT FACTS

Cats love to sleep. On average a cat sleeps between 16 and 18 hours a day!

Cats don't just purr. They make 100 different sounds. Each sound means something different. Do you understand your cat purr-fectly?

Every cat's nose is different. It's like a fingerprint. A cat can be identified by the patterns on its nose.

   86

 A cat can jump six times its height. Remember that when you're leaving your cat alone and don't leave food out (or you might not fur-give yourself!)

 Cats have exceptionally good hearing. They can hear very high-pitched sounds that we can't. A cat's hearing is even better than a dog's.

 A cat uses its whiskers to find out about the things around it. They can sense objects and work out how close they are. Whiskers are especially useful when a cat is moving around in the dark.

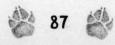

CRAZY CAT WORD CHALLENGE

Unscramble these cat words to find out if you're a top cat or a cat-astrophe!

1. ybatb **2.** ringeg

3. teshellortois

4. hariongl

5. xnma

6. dagollr

ANSWERS ON PAGE 90

    88

ANSWERS TO QUIZ ON PAGES 81–83

1)a 2)b 3)b 4)c 5)a 6)b

     89

ANSWERS TO QUIZ ON PAGE 88

1. Tabby **2.** Ginger **3.** Tortoisehell

4. Longhair **5.** Manx **6.** Ragdoll